Tim AND Sally's

Vegetable Garden

Grady Thrasher

Illustrations by Elaine Hearn Rabon

![d]

HILL STREET PRESS
ATHENS, GEORGIA

❧ A HILL STREET PRESS BOOK ❧

Published in the United States of America by Hill Street Press LLC
191 East Broad Street, Suite 216 • Athens, Georgia 30601-2848 USA

706.713.7200 • info@hillstreetpress.com • www.hillstreetpress.com

Hill Street Press is committed to preserving the written word. Every effort is made to print books on acid-free paper with post-consumer recycled content.

Hill Street Press books are available in bulk purchase and customized editions to institutions and companies. Please contact us for more information.

Illustrations and story copyright ©2007 by H. Grady Thrasher, III

Jacket design and page composition by Jenifer Carter

Printed in the United States

13 Digit ISBN# 978-158818-131-2
10 Digit ISBN# 1-58818-131-6

10 9 8 7 6 5 4 3 2 1

First Printing

This book is dedicated to children and grandchildren everywhere,
and especially Daphne, Brock and Mac.

"Should one ever doubt the existence of miracles, plant a seed and watch it grow."
—the Author

"Though an old man, I am but a young gardener."
—Thomas Jefferson

MAKING A PLAN

Sally and Tim awoke at the break of dawn
and looked out upon their country lawn.

"Look!" Sally said, "How green is the grass
And there's no more frost on the window glass."

Indeed, the cold March winds had blown away
And the April sun rose on a lovely Spring day.

They leapt from their beds in their flannel pajamas
And ran to the bedroom that was Daddy's and Momma's,

While Flip, their large dog at the foot of Tim's bed
Stretched and yawned, then shook his great head.

Have I overslept? thought Flip as he got to his feet,
I'd better run, too! Is it time to eat?

Sally, Tim and Flip (with a last minute leap)
Jumped onto the bed where Mom and Dad were asleep.

"Grump!" mumbled Dad, "I beg your pardon?"
Tim and Sally cried, "Wake up! It's Spring!
We must plant our garden!"

Mom peeked with one eye from her warm, cozy place
Just as Flip's giant tongue started licking her face.

"Hi, Sally. Hi, Tim," Mom said with a grin,
As Flip nuzzled his nose up next to her chin.

"Let's see, it's the weekend, no school bus today,
And we must plant in April to have flowers in May."

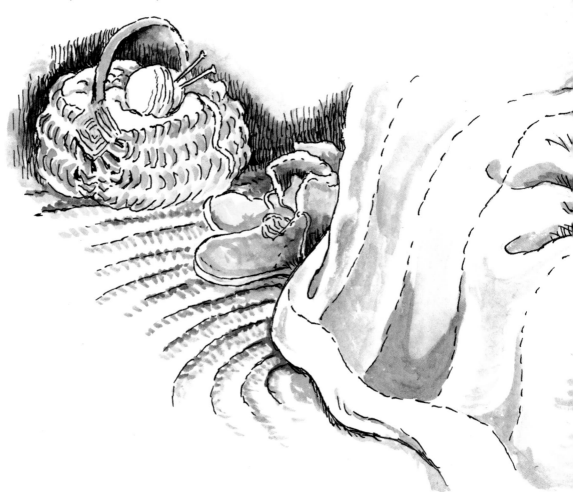

Dad sat up in bed, rubbed sleep from his eyes,
Then looked out and saw the majestic sunrise.

He reached out both arms and, with a couple of tugs,
Embraced Sally and Tim in good morning hugs.

"At the breakfast table, we'll plan what to do;
There's important work ahead for you two!"

The smells of breakfast filled the air
And the table was set with a hearty fare

Of eggs and grits and cereal and jam,
Biscuits, juice and honey-baked ham.

Dad gave thanks for such good food to eat
And for Mom's cooking skills, which were hard to beat.

Flip lay down at Sally's feet
In hopes of being offered a leftover treat.

After second helpings, the meal was done
As the earth warmed outside under morning sun.

Mom said, "When we clear the dishes and wash the pans,
We'll sit back down and make our plans."

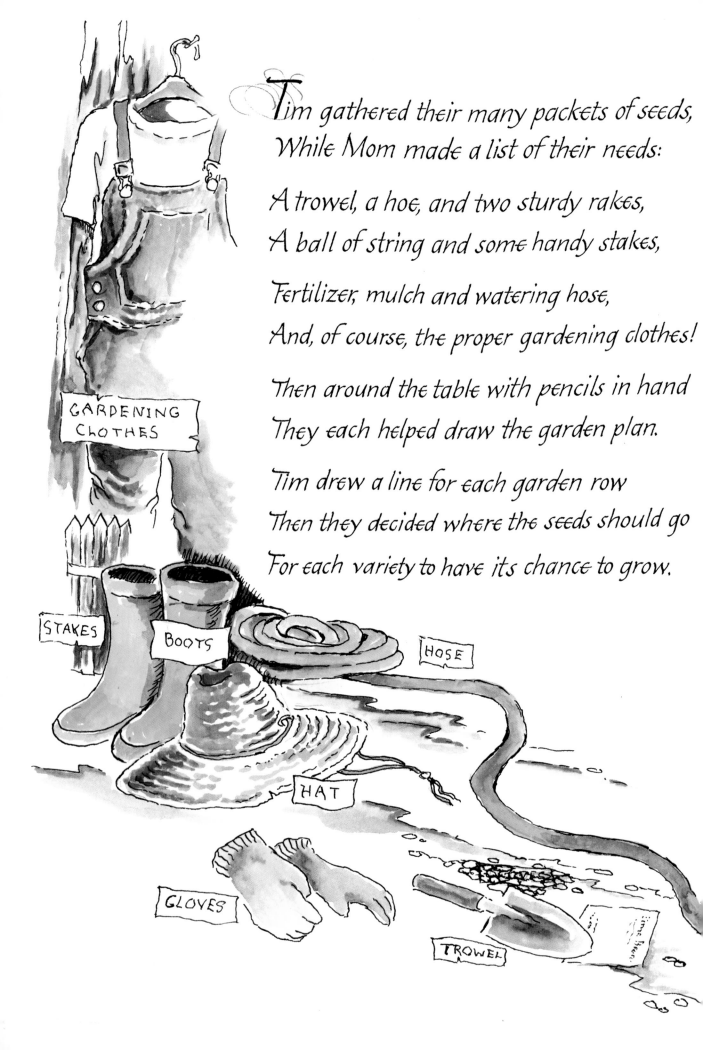

Tim gathered their many packets of seeds,
While Mom made a list of their needs:

A trowel, a hoe, and two sturdy rakes,
A ball of string and some handy stakes,

Fertilizer, mulch and watering hose,
And, of course, the proper gardening clothes!

Then around the table with pencils in hand
They each helped draw the garden plan.

Tim drew a line for each garden row
Then they decided where the seeds should go
For each variety to have its chance to grow.

GARDENING CLOTHES

STAKES

BOOTS

HOSE

HAT

GLOVES

TROWEL

Dad read from his book of gardening lore
Which he had bought at the general store.

"Tall corn to the north to not block out the sun
And give cucumbers space for their vines to run,"

Sally and Tim had seeds for their favorite crops:
For crispy salads, lettuce was tops,

Then corn, spinach and turnip greens,
Cucumbers, carrots and lima beans.

For tomatoes, they had seedlings growing in pots,
Ready to set out in their garden plot.

"Don't forget the flowers," Mom quickly said,
We'll plant all kinds in their own special bed.

With colorful blooms of all variations
For honeybees, it will be a sensation,
They'll help the veggies with pollination.

When the plan was complete, and no detail was missed,
Mom held it up, and it looked like this:

Dad said, "Are we ready to have some fun?
Then let's go outside; there's work to be done!"

Flip scrambled up from his spot on the floor
And was the first one out the kitchen door.

PREPARING THE SOIL

A sunny plot had already been tilled
By Dad during a break in the winter chill.

With some added compost and a little lime
It was almost ready for planting time!

Tim and Sally raked, hoed and worked real hard,
While Flip chased butterflies in the yard.

When the clumps were broken and the soil was fine,
With the stakes and string, they made lines

To follow with the garden hoe
To make straight furrows for each crop row,
Plus hills for cucumber seeds to grow.

Mom said, "My, what a good job you've done!
But it's getting hot here in the sun."

Come, take a break in the shade,
I've made some fresh-squeezed lemonade."

As Mom poured, Dad passed cool drinks around;
Then, refreshed, they lay on the grassy ground

'Neath the swaying limbs of a willow tree,
And felt there was no better place to be.

They listened to some bluebirds sing
And many other sounds of Spring.

Like chirping crickets and buzzing bees
And meadow grass rustling in the breeze.

They looked up into the bright blue sky
And saw geese in formation flying high.

They then heard a huffin', puffin' sound of toil
Like digging in the garden soil.

Digging? Who or what could it be?
They stood up to see what they could see,

And saw that Flip was eagerly trying
To be a gardner, and the dirt was flying!

"Flip," yelled Tim, "That's enough help!"
And Flip leaped toward Tim with a happy yelp,

But his paws got tangled in the strings,
And he rolled over on top of everything

And ended up in a furry ball
Of dirt and strings and stakes and all.

"Well, it looks like we've extra work to do,"
Said Dad, "I'll get a rake and help you two."

And soon rows and stakes were back in place
While Flip resumed his butterfly chase

With a look of pride upon his face
For helping prepare the garden space.

PLANTING

The soil was now ready; it would be evening soon,
And the best time for planting was late afternoon.

"Read carefully instructions that come with the seeds,"
Said Dad, "So we'll know each one's particular needs."

"Plant cucumber seeds a half an inch deep,
Three plants to each hill is all that we'll keep,

So each will have room to grow and spread out
And produce enough cukes to be happy about!

Plant corn in two rows, two feet apart
At a depth of an inch or so would be smart.

Lima beans should be planted the same depth as corn
For large seeds need more soil cover for sprouts to be born.

Now leaf crops like lettuce, spinach and turnip greens, too
Have tiny seeds, so a thin cover will do.

Sow their seeds lightly, then smooth down each row,
And we'll see them sprout in a week or so.

Carrots and radishes are different crops,
For we eat their roots, instead of their tops.

Plant those seeds one-half inch down and a half inch apart
So when they sprout, roots will have room from the start."
Mom said, "To help remember all this, I've made us a chart."

PLANTING CHART

Vegetable	Depth of Seed	Thin to between plants
Lettuce —	1/8 inch	4 - 6 inches
Spinach —	1/2 inch	2 - 4 inches
Turnip Greens —	1/2 inch	2 - 3 inches
Lima beans —	1 inch	6 inches
Carrots —	1/4 inch	3 inches
Corn —	1 inch	6 - 8 inches
Radishes —	1/2 inch	1 inch

Tim and Sally worked hard like busy little ants,
And soon, all was done except the tomato plants.

Tim scooped holes six inches deep and one foot around,
While Sally carefully placed each plant in the ground.

She covered roots and stem with the well-prepared dirt
And their tops with paper so hot sun wouldn't hurt.

Mom said, "They're tender now, but soon they'll be strong
And will enjoy full sun all the day long."

Tim and Sally soon finished, and they stood side by side
To look at their garden with satisfaction and pride.

Dad attached the sprinkler to the garden hose
And turned it on softly to wet down the rows.

The setting sun made the western sky red
As they gathered their tools to place in the shed.

Mom said, "We did it! Fresh veggies soon will be ours,
And tomorrow we'll plant seeds for some beautiful flowers."

Dad said, "Your garden surely will be a winner;
Now, let's go in the house and wash up for dinner."

Soon after dinner, Tim and Sally were asleep,
Each dreaming of bountiful harvests to reap.

While Flip on Tim's bed breathed sleepy dog sighs,
As dreams of butterflies sailed past his eyes.

THE GARDEN GROWS

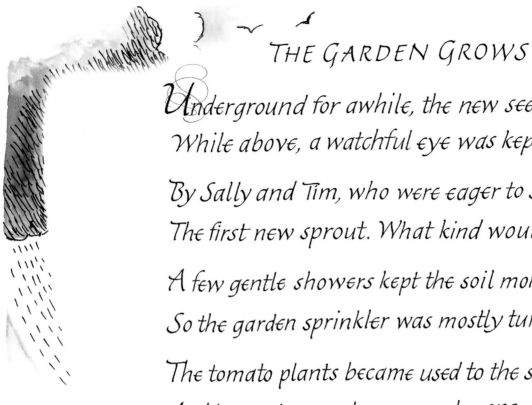

Underground for awhile, the new seeds slept
While above, a watchful eye was kept

By Sally and Tim, who were eager to see
The first new sprout. What kind would it be?

A few gentle showers kept the soil moist and soft
So the garden sprinkler was mostly turned off.

The tomato plants became used to the sun
And began to grow large, one by one.

Sally and Tim daily examined each row
To see which seeds had started to grow.

One day after school, they exclaimed with glee,
"Dad and Mom! You must come and see!"

On that bright afternoon Tim and Sally found
A hundred new shoots had poked through the ground.

Mom said, "You've given them all a good start
And now Mother Nature is doing her part.

For awhile we'll care for each growing sprout,
But in a few days we must thin them out,
So their roots will have room to spread all about

And gather water and minerals from the soil below
To provide each plant with what's needed to grow."

And during the spring, the plants did just that,
And by June the corn was as high as Dad's hat.

Each day after school, Tim and Sally pulled weeds
And tended to each crop's own special needs.

The tomatoes required stakes to hold them upright
And to be watched closely for insects or blight.

A little fertilizer applied here and there
Helped strengthen the plants for the fruit they would bear.

The cucumber vines spread out in their space,
And soon little cukes were all over the place,

As well as turnip greens and lima beans,
And carrot root tops soon could be seen.

The corn stalks grew tassels, then ears on each stalk,
Tim and Sally would count them between rows as they walked.

Now school was out, it was summer vacation
And each day was filled with great expectation.

Mom's flowers were blooming with colors so fair,
And the buzzing of bees filled the warm, perfumed air.

Flip, happy Tim and Sally were home every day,
Awoke with them early to go out and play.

Then he'd run through the yard, chasing a stick,
While they checked the garden for vegetables to pick.

Every day before breakfast each mild summer morn
They'd fill baskets with tomatoes and ears of sweet corn

And cucumbers, carrots and lima beans,
Plus lettuce, spinach and turnip greens!

Because of their preparation, hard work and care,
An abundant harvest allowed them to share

Their fresh produce with neighbors and friends,
And still the vegetables kept coming in!

They had tomato sandwiches and succotash stew,
Corn on the cob and off the cob, too!

Lettuce with cucumbers sliced in a group,
And Mom made gallons of vegetable soup.

Tim and Sally were amazed that such little seeds
Could create so much, fill so many needs.

They asked Mom and Dad, "How could this be true?"
Mom said, "Your wonderful garden has taught each of you,

With each plump tomato and bursting bean pod,
That gardeners work in partnership with God."

THE
END

WORD LIST

seeds

corn

carrots

cucumbers

lima beans

spinach

WORD LIST

lettuce

tomatoes

radishes

turnip

bluebird

honeybee

WORD LIST

butterfly

basket

cricket

garden hoe

gloves

rake

WORD LIST

hat

shovel

hose

stakes and string

trowel

wheelbarrow

GARDEN JOURNAL

Igive special thanks to Bonnie Ramsey for her
recommendation of Elaine Rabon as illustrator,
to Kenneth Williams for his fine lettering,
to Kay McMorrow for her assistance
and durable enthusiasm, and to my wife,
Kathy Prescott, for everything.

—Grady Thrasher

The Publisher offers special thanks to Donna Carney,
and all the fine folks at Barrow Elementary School
in Athens, Georgia, as well as
Janice Shay for her consultation on this project.